Mr. King's Castle

For my parents, Lucie and Roland — G.C.

Kids Can Press acknowledges the financial support of the Government of Ontario, through the Ontario Media Development Corporation's Ontario Book Initiative; the Ontario Arts Council; the Canada Council for the Arts; and the Government of Canada, through the CBF, for our publishing activity.

Published in Canada by
Kids Can Press Ltd.
25 Dockside Drive
Toronto, ON M5A 0B5

Published in the U.S. by
Kids Can Press Ltd.
2250 Military Road
Tonawanda, NY 14150

www.kidscanpress.com

Kids Can Press is a *Corus*™ Entertainment company

The artwork in this book was rendered in multi-media. The text is set in Futura Book.

Edited by Karen Li and Stacey Roderick
Designed by Karen Powers and Julia Naimska

This book is smyth sewn casebound.
Manufactured in China, in 3/2013, through
Asia Pacific Offset

CM 13 0 9 8 7 6 5 4 3 2 1

Library and Archives Canada Cataloguing in Publication

Côté, Geneviève, 1964–

Mr. King's castle / written and illustrated by Geneviève Côté.

(Mr. King)
ISBN 978-1-55453-972-7

    I. Title.
PS8605.O8738M56 2013   jC813'.6   C2012-908287-2

Geneviève Côté

Mr. King's Castle

KIDS CAN PRESS

Mr. King lives on top of a **BIG** hill.

He wants to build himself a **BIG** castle.

Mr. King likes **BIG** things.

CHOP! CHOP! CHOP!

Mr. King starts chopping off
blocks to build his castle. He
is too busy to notice the BIG
holes he is leaving behind.

CHOP! CHOP! CHOP!

Mr. King's friends come running.
"What is that NOISE?"

"What are these HOLES?"

"What are these BLOCKS?"

Mr. King is too busy to hear them.
Block by block, bit by bit, his castle is
getting BIGGER and BIGGER.

Mr. King chops until there is nothing left to chop and builds until there is nothing left to build with.

Then he stops and proudly looks out the window.

"Hmm … there isn't much of a view," says Mr. King.

Down below, his friends are grumbling.

"What happened to the hill?" ask Bert and Tex.

"What happened to my favorite napping spot?" asks Harriet.

"Where are the flowers?"
wonders Old Jim Elk.

"What happened
to the grass I eat?"
asks P.J.

"And where is our
secret stash of nuts?!"
cry Skit and Skat.

One by one, they gather
under the castle window.

Everyone is staring at
Mr. King, and suddenly
he feels very small.

"Uh-oh. That was a **BIG**
mistake," he says after a
while. "Maybe I should put
everything back."

"YAY!!" All his friends jump up to help.

Together they start taking down the BIG castle,
block by block, bit by bit.

And block by block, bit by bit, they put everything back just like it was before.

… Well, ALMOST like it was before.

"There is one piece left," says Mr. King. "But I don't see where it fits. What shall we do with it?"

After whispering to the others, Tex says:
"Close your eyes. We have an idea."

When Mr. King opens his eyes,
his friends sing out "SURPRISE!!"

Tonight, in his small castle,
Mr. King is going to have
a **BIG** party!